The Girls of the Good Day Orphanage

Kate
⏰ Be Late ⏰

by CAROL BEACH YORK

illustrated by Victoria de Larrea

cover illustration by John Speirs

A
LITTLE APPLE
PAPERBACK

SCHOLASTIC INC.

New York   Toronto   London   Auckland   Sydney

For Diana
with my love

No part of this publication may be reproduced in whole or in
part, or stored in a retrieval system, or transmitted in any
form or by any means, electronic, mechanical, photocopying,
recording, or otherwise, without written permission of the
publisher. For information regarding permission, write to
Scholastic Inc., 555 Broadway, New York, NY 10012.

ISBN 0-590-40056-8

12 11 10 9 8 7 6 5 4 3 2 1   4 5 6 7 8 9/9

Printed in the U.S.A.   40

Contents

Kate Be Late

❉ It was a warm summer day. Bees hung over the flowerbeds in the gardens of the houses in Butterfield Square, and a breeze stirred gently in the treetops.

At Number 18, THE GOOD DAY ORPHANAGE FOR GIRLS, the handyman was mowing the grass, a bright blue handkerchief flapping from his back pocket. Little girls played here and there around the yard. On the front steps, a red-haired girl named Mary was sitting with a notebook open in her lap. She was making up poems. It was just the day for it.

Little Ann,
Little Ann,
Saw a bee
And away she ran!

"Very good," said Mary to herself.

She turned to a fresh page and began again:

Sally is silly,
Sally is wise,
Sally eats cookies
And coconut pies!

"Even better," said Mary to herself.

She counted back over the pages and saw that she had written five poems already this morning. It was time to read them to somebody — which is half the fun of writing poems.

She looked around the yard to see if there was anyone around who would like her poems.

Agnes was reading a book under a tree. Agnes did not like to be interrupted when she was reading.

Nonnie and Elizabeth were playing tag.

The other girls had run around to the back, following the handyman and the *whirrr* of his mower.

There was Elsie May, of course. She was standing by the gate twisting a long braid between her fingers. But Mary did not think she wanted to read her poems to Elsie May. Elsie May was too stuck-up.

Mary ran up the steps, opened the front door, and looked down the hallway that led to the parlor. Everything was quiet inside. The hall floor gleamed from a fresh waxing, and a bowl of yellow daisies stood on a table by the stairway.

Mary went along the polished floor, past the fresh, bright daisies, in search of someone to read her poems to. At the parlor doorway she stopped and stuck in her head. Ah! Miss Lavender and Miss Plum were there together, and they did not look too busy. Miss Lavender

was only doing the mending, her sewing basket beside her on the sofa, her needle flashing in the sunlight. And Miss Plum was only sitting at her desk writing. They would certainly like to stop and hear some poems, Mary was sure.

"Come in, Mary."

Miss Lavender had seen the little red-head in the doorway, and she smiled and patted the sofa cushion beside her.

"Come and tell me what you've been doing all morning."

"I've been writing poems," Mary said.

Mary held out her notebook proudly and went to the sofa to sit down. She squeezed right in between Miss Lavender and the sewing basket. Miss Lavender set down her mending and said, "Writing poems? Isn't that nice. Will you read some to me?"

Miss Plum turned from her desk, still holding her pen over the paper. She was going to listen, too.

Miss Plum and Miss Lavender took care

of The Good Day girls. They did everything from seeing that the girls had warm mittens in winter to listening to poems on summer days.

Mary opened her book to page one and began:

> *"Sue likes yellow,*
> *Sue likes blue,*
> *Sue likes me*
> *And Sue likes you!"*

"Why that's lovely," Miss Lavender exclaimed. "Isn't that lovely, Miss Plum?"

"Lovely," Miss Plum agreed.

> *"Nonnie had a nickel,*
> *Nonnie had a dime,*
> *Nonnie had a lot of money*
> *All the time!"*

Miss Lavender laughed.

"How true that is," she said.

Of all the little Good Day girls, Nonnie

was the most careful with her money. She had a penny jar, and she saved every penny she could find. Sometimes she walked down the street and over to the park in the Square, just looking for pennies that had dropped out of people's pockets.

Mary glowed under this praise. She did not need any encouragement to read some more of her poems.

"Kate be early,
Kate be late,
Kate jump over
The garden gate!"

Miss Lavender laughed again.

"My, that one's true, too, isn't it. I never saw a girl who liked to jump over things the way Kate does."

Miss Plum smiled faintly. True, indeed. Kate was always jumping over gates instead of walking through. She was always climbing trees and standing on her head.

But Miss Plum's thoughts about Kate

were interrupted as Mary began to read her next poem.

"Little Ann,
Little Ann,
Saw a bee
And away she ran!"

Miss Lavender was really laughing now. Little Ann was only five years old and every bug she saw was a bee. "A bee is chasing me," she would cry, and whenever anyone ran to see, it was always just a pesky fly, or a tiny mosquito. Once she found a beetle crawling up the front walk, and she had called all the other girls to come and see the "bee."

Mary read the poem about Sally eating cookies and coconut pies, and Miss Lavender said: "I think we will have to put Sally on a diet one of these days!"

"That's all I've got so far today," Mary said.

She closed her notebook and smiled up into Miss Lavender's plump face. Above the plump face, rows of white curls crowned Miss Lavender's head. If Mary looked closely, sometimes she could see hairpins sticking here and there amid the curls.

Miss Plum was silent for a moment. Then she said, "Read us that one about Kate again."

Mary ruffled through the pages of her book.

"Kate be early,
Kate be late,
Kate jump over
The garden gate!"

"Yes . . ." Miss Plum murmured to herself. "Well, thank you for reading the poems to us, Mary. Now I see it is time for you to wash for lunch."

When Mary had gone, Miss Lavender began to put her mending away in the basket.

But Miss Plum sat thoughtfully at her desk. She set her pen down and stared absently at the papers before her. Mary's poems were all so true, and the one about

Kate was the truest of all. *Kate be late.*

Kate always had her mind on a hundred other things besides what she was supposed to be doing and where she was supposed to be. She was always rushing in late for meals, and rushing out late for school. More and more in the past weeks Miss Plum had noticed that Kate was getting worse and worse. Last week, they had all almost missed the bus for the picnic at Elm Hill because Kate was late!

Miss Plum sighed softly to herself and at last stood up. It was time for lunch now. But it was also time, she thought, for a talk with Kate. Perhaps after lunch. After all, it was not a good habit to get into, always being late. And Miss Plum liked The Good Day girls to have good habits.

Miss Plum went into the dining room with Miss Lavender. Soon twenty-seven little girls with washed hands and combed hair were sitting at the table — but where was Kate? Miss Plum was not surprised when Kate came running in last.

It was happening more and more often. And something must be done.

"Something must be done about Kate," Miss Plum said softly to Miss Lavender.

"Yes, of course," Miss Lavender agreed, taking a muffin from a plate that was going by. Miss Lavender always agreed with everything Miss Plum said, and Miss Plum was always right.

A Talk
With Miss Plum

✳ After lunch, Miss Plum asked Kate to come into the parlor for a few minutes.

All the other girls scattered away like puffs blown from a dandelion stalk. Two went to the kitchen to help Cook with the dishes. Some went outdoors to play and watch the handyman clipping the hedges. Agnes had a new book to read, and Phoebe was making a bracelet out of colored beads.

Kate had planned to go next door with Tatty and Mary to see the Bennett family's new kittens. She was very disappointed to be told to come into the parlor instead. She sat on the edge of a chair and wondered if Tatty and Mary would wait for her.

"Now Kate," Miss Plum began, "I've been meaning to talk to you about your running into the dining room late for meals. It's happening nearly every day."

Kate looked at the carpet.

She was a strong little girl with dark hair and eyes. She wished she had been born a boy, but she could not help being a girl. She was eight years old, and she liked to climb trees and walk fence rails and jump gates. Today she had been trying to learn to walk on her hands. That was why she was late to lunch. But she didn't think Miss Plum would think much of that excuse.

Miss Plum sat at her desk, the chair turned around so that she could face Kate squarely.

Miss Lavender sat on the sofa and began to get out her mending things again. Her usually smiling face was very serious. She knew it was right for Miss Plum to speak to

Kate. But still it was always hard for Miss Lavender when one of the girls had to be scolded.

"And several times before school ended you were tardy at school, too," Miss Plum continued. "You remember that, don't you, Kate?"

"Yes."

"And last week, when we were all ready to leave for the picnic and the bus was about to go, you were late. We nearly missed the bus. That would have meant we would have missed the picnic. All of us. All the other girls."

"Yes."

"You must try to do better, dear," Miss Plum said. Her tone softened a bit. Kate looked so crestfallen, her head drooping, her eyes fastened on the floor.

Kate nodded uncomfortably.

"Being on time is a courtesy to others, you know," Miss Plum said. "And besides being a courtesy, it is an orderly way to live."

Kate nodded again. She was wondering if Tatty and Mary had gone on ahead to look at the kittens.

"Now you must promise me to try to do better in the future." Miss Plum took Kate's chin and tilted it up so that she was looking straight into Kate's face.

"I will," Kate said. She stared into Miss Plum's deep gray eyes.

"All right then," Miss Plum said. "You may go and play now. And Kate — " she added, as Kate scrambled up and started for the door, " — Kate, try to be on time for supper tonight."

Kate smiled. Supper was hours away. First she had to hurry and see the new kittens.

"Now I know everything will be all right," Miss Lavender said, when Kate had gone. "All she needed was a little reminding."

"I hope you're right." Miss Plum smiled thoughtfully. "I hope you're right."

Miss Lavender bit off her thread and

began to hum to herself. Soon she had forgotten all about Kate-be-late.

But Miss Plum did not forget. And as suppertime got near, she began to think even more about Kate. She saw girls coming in and starting to wash for supper. She heard voices and clattering shoes in the hall. She hoped one of those pairs of clattering shoes belonged to Kate.

But at six o'clock there were only twenty-seven little girls in the dining room.

The Treasure Box

✳ "Shall we start without Kate?" Miss Lavender whispered to Miss Plum.

Miss Plum sighed. All the other girls were waiting for their supper. It was not their fault Kate was late.

"Yes," Miss Plum said. "We will start without her."

Five minutes went by. Then ten minutes. All the other girls were eating and still no Kate. At last Miss Plum heard the front door open and the sound of feet running along the hall — but not toward the dining room. The footsteps started upstairs.

"Excuse me, please," Miss Plum murmured, and got up from her chair.

She reached the hallway just in time to see Kate at the top of the stairs.

"Kate!" she called up to her.

Kate turned and looked down at Miss Plum. Her face was bright with excitement. "Oh — Miss Plum, I was just going to show Phoebe what I found for my treasure box."

Miss Plum walked to the foot of the stairs. She could see that Kate had a cardboard shoe box in her arms.

"Phoebe is not upstairs," Miss Plum said sternly.

"She's not?"

"Phoebe is in the dining room eating her dinner."

"Oh."

All the excitement left Kate's face. Suppertime had come, and she was late again!

"Come down, please," Miss Plum said.

Slowly, step by step, Kate started down the stairs, carrying her shoe box.

"You may show me whatever it was that

was so important that you are late again for a meal," Miss Plum said.

Kate opened the shoe box. Inside, Miss Plum could see an odd jumble of things, on top of which lay something that looked like a doorknob.

"What is all this stuff?" Miss Plum asked.

She poked into the shoe box. There were several large green and blue marbles. A top. A single gold earring. And a lot of other strange objects.

"It's my treasure box," Kate answered shyly. Her eyes met Miss Plum's. "I've been collecting it all summer."

"And this is why you were late for dinner tonight?"

"I found the doorknob just as I was coming along the street." Kate's eyes began to shine a little as she picked up the old brass doorknob and held it out for Miss Plum to see.

"It was lying by the curb. It didn't belong to anybody. I wanted to show it to Phoebe. . . ."

Kate's voice trailed off. Phoebe. . . . Phoebe

was in the dining room, eating her supper. That was where Kate herself ought to have been.

Miss Plum looked into the shoe box again. She saw a wooden clothespin with a face drawn on its top, a tiny china cat with a chipped ear, a long strand of pink velvet ribbon, a large slightly rusty key.

"I think I will keep the treasure box for a while," Miss Plum said.

Kate's eyes widened with surprise and distress.

Miss Plum took the shoe box and put on the lid. She saw that Kate had written on the cover with a black crayon:

MY TREASURE BOX

"I'm sorry to have to do this, Kate — but you must learn to think of others," Miss Plum said. "When you have proved to me that you can be more prompt, you may have this back again."

Kate stared at Miss Plum silently, and Miss Plum sighed.

"Now go and wash your hands and comb your hair and come have your dinner."

What Is Needed

※ Poor Kate. She got into her bed very sadly that night. All her "treasures" were gone. All her summer's collecting. She had not even been able to show Phoebe the beautiful brass doorknob. She lay awake, staring into the darkness, and two bright tears came into her eyes. She had found the pink ribbon caught on a bush in the park, the gold earring lying in a puddle after a rain storm. . . .

She would have to earn back her treasure box.

She must! It was the most important thing she owned.

She would never be late again!

The next morning Kate was the first girl dressed, and she was downstairs in the dining room half an hour before breakfast.

"What are you doing up so early?" Cook asked.

She was setting spoons and napkins on the table, and there sat Kate, ready in her chair.

"I just woke up early," Kate said.

But Cook thought she knew better. She knew Kate was usually late to meals, and Cook thought something was up.

"As long as you're here, you might as well come out in the kitchen and help me make the oatmeal," Cook suggested. She thought it would be a long time for Kate to sit and wait until breakfast was ready.

Miss Plum and Miss Lavender were delighted to see Kate already in the dining room when they came in. Five or six other girls had come down by then, and at exactly eight o'clock, breakfast time, there were twenty-eight girls in twenty-eight chairs around the table.

Little Ann, piling sugar on her oatmeal.

Elsie May with hairbows on her braids.

Tatty, looking a little neater than usual because she had combed her hair back out of her eyes and gotten the buttons of her dress buttoned into the right buttonholes.

Red-haired Mary (perhaps more poems swirling in her mind).

Phoebe with a homemade bead bracelet sliding on her arm.

And all the rest.

Even Kate.

"This is just the way it should be," Miss Plum said, and she smiled encouragingly at Kate.

Kate was filled with hope. Maybe now she could have her treasure box back.

It was Kate's turn to help with dishes, so she could not speak to Miss Plum as quickly as she wanted. But as soon as she had dried the last teaspoon for Cook, and put the last milk glass into the cupboard, she ran down the hall to the parlor. Miss Plum and Miss Lavender were sitting on the sofa.

Kate was halfway across the room when she caught sight of another figure by the window. It was Mr. Not So Much, one of the members of the Board of Directors of The Good Day. He stood glowering darkly out of the window at the golden summer day. His bony hands were crossed behind his back, and his gold watch chain sparkled in the sunlight.

"What is it Kate?" Miss Plum said. At the sound of her voice, Mr. Not So Much turned from glowering out the window and glowered at Kate instead.

Kate was speechless. Any Good Day girl would have been, in the presence of the dreadful Mr. Not So Much. He came once a month to discuss the expenses of the orphanage with Miss Plum. And he always found a great many things wrong.

He always found that Miss Plum and Miss Lavender were spending too much money!

It upset him to see the squandering of money, but there was no help for it. Someone must come and look over the bills, and the job had fallen to him. It was a duty he performed grimly, and Miss Plum and Miss Lavender were not the only ones who gave him trouble. He could always be sure Cook was in the kitchen wasting precious money on unnecessary food — cakes, cookies, muffins. It was really more than Mr. Not So Much could bear, to think of Cook in her kitchen.

Kate wanted to run right out of the parlor again when she saw Mr. Not So Much, but she caught sight of her treasure box on the edge of Miss Plum's desk. Inside was the gold earring, the top that would spin if she could only find a long string, her beautiful marbles. And the brass doorknob.

"What is it, Kate?" Miss Plum asked again. She was glad of any interruption when Mr. Not So Much came. His visits were as hard on her as they were on him.

"I came for my treasure box," Kate said.

"I think I must keep it awhile yet, Kate. One breakfast does not seem proof to me that you have learned your lesson."

"What's this now?" Mr. Not So Much demanded to know.

Miss Plum hesitated a moment. She did not want to embarrass Kate by answering Mr. Not So Much, but there seemed nothing else to do. She couldn't say it was none of his business, since The Good Day girls *were* his business. They were the concern of all the members of the Board of Directors.

"Kate has been having a little trouble getting to places on time," Miss Plum said at last. "She is trying to do better."

Kate's face flamed red with embarrassment to have herself discussed under the steady stare of Mr. Not So Much.

"I see." Mr. Not So Much took one bony hand from behind his back and pulled at his chin. Next to wasting money, wasting time was second on his list of sins.

"The value of time, young lady," he said to Kate, "cannot be overestimated. Time is money."

"Yes, sir," Kate mumbled, flushing redder than ever.

Mr. Not So Much pulled out his gold watch and held it in his hand. He was very proud of his watch, and its steady tick ruled every hour of his day. *He* was never late anywhere.

"Can you read time?" he asked, holding his watch toward Kate.

"Yes, sir."

"Then why are you not on time?"

Kate had no answer for this. She twisted her fingers together miserably and looked over to Miss Lavender for help.

"Are you late to school?" Mr. Not So Much asked.

"Sometimes," Kate answered in a very tiny voice.

"And are you late to meals?"

"Sometimes."

"Are you late for appointments?"

Miss Lavender laughed nervously. "I don't think Kate has many 'appointments,' do you, dear?"

Kate could only twist her fingers tighter together. She had had an appointment to go with Tatty and Mary to see the new kittens only yesterday, and they had gone on without her because Miss Plum had called her into the parlor.

Yes, Kate had to admit to herself, she did not have many "appointments." But when she did, she was late for them. She didn't *mean* to be late. Things just seemed to turn out that way.

With horror, she saw that Mr. Not So Much had begun to drum his fingers on the

top of her treasure box. What if he should take it away with him to punish her...?

But Mr. Not So Much did not even notice what his fingers were tapping upon. He had other thoughts in his mind, and after a moment he said:

"I think I know what is needed here."

Kate shuddered. She was sure it would be something awful if Mr. Not So Much thought of it.

"And what is that?" Miss Plum asked calmly.

"You will see," he said mysteriously. "But Kate must come with me for a few minutes."

"Oh," said Miss Plum.

"Oh," said Miss Lavender.

Poor Kate was so frightened she could not even speak.

The 2$ Special

✳ Kate trotted along the street, trying to keep up with Mr. Not So Much. His steps were twice as long as hers. She was nearly running.

He did not speak a word to her, or look back to see if she was still trotting after him.

About three blocks from The Good Day, Mr. Not So Much stopped at last in front of a store.

And then he did speak.

He frowned down at Kate and said, "What's needed is a watch for you to wear. Nobody can rightly tell what they're doing without a watch."

He patted the gold chain which swung from his pocket.

Before Kate could answer, he opened the door and stalked into the shop. Kate trotted along behind him.

At a counter near the back of the store, Mr. Not So Much found what he wanted — a display of clocks and wristwatches. A young man stood behind the counter. As Mr. Not So Much walked up to him, he said brightly, "Good morning, sir. What may I do for you?"

"I doubt there is anything you could do for me," Mr. Not So Much announced. He stared down at the display of watches under the glass countertop. His own beautiful gold watch was far superior to any of these.

"The person you may help is this young lady here."

The clerk leaned across the counter and saw Kate peering out from behind Mr. Not So Much.

"And what can we do for the young lady?" the clerk asked.

"She needs a wristwatch," Mr. Not So

Much said. And then he added quickly, "One of your less expensive ones."

"Now let's see what we have." The young man reached in under the glass and took out a tray of watches labeled $7.95.

"Seven dollars and ninety-five cents?" Mr. Not So Much did not even look at the watches. The price card was enough for him to know these were not the watches *he* wanted.

"Too much, sir?" the clerk asked politely. "Then let me see — we do have a few for five dollars. And yes, I think there is one of our two dollar specials left — ah yes — "

He fumbled around in the display case a moment and produced one watch with a $5.00 price tag and another watch with a big red tag that said 2$ SPECIAL.

Mr. Not So Much wasted no time on the five-dollar watch. He picked up the 2$ Special and rubbed it between his long thin fingers. It looked like a good enough watch to him.

"Will it run?" he asked the clerk.

"All our watches run, sir," the young man replied.

"Hmmm." Mr. Not So Much turned over the 2$ Special and peered at the back.

"Of course, you do get what you pay for," the clerk reminded him. "Now this five-dollar watch has been one of our best sellers."

Mr. Not So Much looked at the young man suspiciously. He had made up his mind already to take the 2$ Special, and he did not want to hear anything about five-dollar watches. He did not throw away his money like *some* people.

As Kate and the clerk watched, Mr. Not So Much wound the watch stem between his thumb and forefinger. *"Grrr-grrr-grrr"* came the faint winding sound. Then he drew out his own gold pocket watch and noted the time: exactly ten o'clock. He replaced his own watch carefully in his pocket and set the hands of the 2$ Special to ten o'clock.

Then he turned and said to Kate, "Hold out your arm."

Kate lifted her arm, somewhat mosquito-bitten since she had been practicing standing on her hands in the long grass behind the back fence. She certainly wished she were there now — or hanging from one of the branches of the apple tree she so much loved to climb.

Mr. Not So Much leaned forward and put the watch band around Kate's wrist. He adjusted it to the right size, slipped the buckle into place, and straightened up with an air of satisfaction. Two dollars. It was hard for him to part with money, but he had gotten off better then he expected.

Even so, he paid the clerk grudgingly, and his mouth tightened when he saw his dollar bills disappear forever into the store cash register.

Kate held the watch to her ear and listened to its pleasant tick-tick-tick.

"Now you have your watch," said Mr. Not So Much. He was sure this would solve all Kate's problems.

He walked rapidly out of the store and headed toward The Good Day. Time was money, and he had already spent all he could spare of both.

Kate ran along behind Mr. Not So Much. She lifted her wrist now and then to listen to the ticking.

But they had not gone far when the watch became silent. Kate shook her arm and pressed the watch close to her ear.

But it was quite silent. There was no longer any tick-tick-tick to be heard from the 2$ Special.

"Mr. Not So Much — " Kate called, as she scurried along behind him. "Mr. Not So Much — "

"You have your watch. You need never be late again."

"But Mr. Not So Much — "

He made an impatient motion. "Not so

much talking," he said. "Children should be seen and not heard." This was one of his favorite mottos.

Mr. Not So Much increased his stride to an even faster pace. Kate had little breath left to try to talk to him, even if she dared.

At The Good Day, Mr. Not So Much was disappointed to find Miss Plum and Miss Lavender gone. The only person in the parlor was a plump girl practicing the piano.

"Where are the ladies?" Mr. Not So Much demanded.

"They went to do errands," the plump girl said shyly. She was Sally, who ate cookies and coconut pies in Mary's poem. She hoped Mr. Not So Much was not going to sit down in the parlor to wait for the ladies to return. How could she practice the piano with Mr. Not So Much so close? She would not hit one right note, she was sure.

Mr. Not So Much had no intention of wasting any more time. He wheeled around, nearly falling over Kate who was huddled at his side. As he strode to the front door, she trailed after him uncertainly. As he opened the door he frowned down at her. Kate's tongue stuck in her mouth. She could not say one word about the 2$ Special.

"I must be on my way," Mr. Not So Much said. "When the ladies return, you may show them your watch. I will be back in a week to see if you have improved your ways."

With that he was gone. Kate sat down on the front step to wait for Miss Lavender and Miss Plum. She didn't think they were going to be very excited about a watch that didn't even tick.

From the back yard she could hear laughter as some of The Good Day girls played hide-and-seek. From the open parlor window came the plunking notes of the piano.

Kate tried winding her watch, but it did not want to be wound. The stem was already tight. The hands stood motionless at eight minutes past ten. It looked like they were there to stay forever.

Nonnie's News

✳ If Mr. Not So Much had stayed awhile longer, he would have seen a sight to warm his heart — Nonnie and her money jar. Kate had been sitting on the front step only a few minutes when Nonnie came up the walk rattling her whole summer's collection of coins in her glass jar. She had been around the neighborhood and in the park in the Square, and it had been a very successful trip.

She had found a penny on a sidewalk curb and a quarter by the little stone fountain in the park.

Yes, Mr. Not So Much would have been

pleased to see such a girl as Nonnie, hard at work collecting money.

Nonnie didn't know anything about Kate's problems. As soon as she caught sight of Kate she rushed up to her, bursting with news:

"Guess what I saw! A carnival — over on Willow Street. Let's go, Kate. We can ride on the merry-go-round and buy cotton candy."

Kate looked up at Nonnie. She began to forget about what an awful morning she was having.

"I was walking along looking for money, and there was the carnival," Nonnie said. "But I didn't want to go in alone. Come on, Kate, come with me."

Nonnie was a thin girl, tall for her age, with bony knees and elbows. She ate as much as everybody else, but she was always thin. This morning she had tied her hair back with a long piece of purple ribbon, and she looked just right for a carnival.

Kate got up from the step. A carnival sounded very exciting, but she hesitated. "I don't have any money."

"I'll share." Nonnie held up her glass jar proudly. "I have lots of money."

The two girls were racing down the front walk when Elsie May came walking along. "Whoa!" she said, catching hold of the closest arm, which was Kate's. "Where are you running off to so fast?"

Elsie May was the oldest Good Day girl. She was very bossy, and she always wanted to know everything, even things that were not her business.

"We're going to the carnival," Nonnie said. She held her glass jar close to her side. Elsie May had often said she thought Nonnie was silly to carry an old jelly jar around all summer.

"Did you ask if you can go?" Elsie May said.

"Miss Plum and Miss Lavender aren't here right now," Kate said. She pulled away from Elsie May and ran on down the walk with Nonnie.

"You could ask Cook," Elsie May called after them.

When they didn't stop, she called out again:

"I'll tell. I'll tell that you went without asking."

A Yellow Elephant

✳ The carnival was set up in a large empty lot on Willow Street, just as Nonnie had said. Kate could hardly believe she was seeing such a marvelous thing so close to home. Strings of brightly colored flags fluttered overhead in the warm summer breeze. Merry-go-round music tinkled. Fastened between two tall poles was a big red banner with white letters a foot high:

SUMMER CARNIVAL
EVERYBODY WELCOME

"Does it cost money to go in?" Kate asked, as they came to a stop by the sign.

Nonnie didn't know. They stood for a moment admiring the wonderful carnival just beyond the poles and the red sign.

"Ice-cold lemonade. Ice-cold lemonade. Ten cents a cup. Step right this way, ladies." A roly-poly man carrying a tray of paper cups beckoned to Nonnie and Kate, and they walked right into the carnival. It didn't cost even one penny to get in.

Nonnie opened her jar and found two dimes for two cups of lemonade. It was a very warm morning, and they had run all the way. They needed something cool to drink. The cups were not very large, and Kate drank her lemonade in one gulp.

The lemonade man went on his way. "Ice-cold lemonade. Get your ice-cold lemonade."

There was so much to see, Kate and Nonnie didn't know where to begin. People streamed by. There were sunburned boys with mustard on their cheeks from eating hot dogs, little girls with sticks of cotton candy, mothers clutching toddlers firmly by the hand. Some people had dolls and fancy canes and stuffed toys they had won at the game booths.

"Try your luck, ladies?" A man leaned across the counter of his booth as Kate and Nonnie came by. "Toss the rings, win the prizes. Three rings only a quarter."

But Kate and Nonnie wandered on. They wanted to see everything and pick just the right things to spend their money on.

"Red hots, red hots," a voice was calling, "Get your red hots here!"

The balloon man had a hundred balloons floating over his head, and children crowded around a clown walking on stilts. Kate looked up and there, far above, was the face of the clown grinning down at her.

"Let's ride the merry-go-round," Nonnie said at last, after they had walked around awhile to see everything.

They went toward the tinkling music, where children were riding orange giraffes and yellow elephants and blue horses.

"I think I'll ride a giraffe," Nonnie said. They stood watching the merry-go-round. "What do you want to ride?"

Kate wanted to ride them all! An orange giraffe and a blue horse and a yellow elephant ... or maybe a pink camel with a bright gold saddle between its humps. How could she decide?

The merry-go-round was slowing down. The music stopped and the children got off.

"Ride the merry-go-round. Step this way for your tickets!"

Nonnie and Kate got into line and Nonnie poked around in her jar for quarters. Her purple hair ribbon had slipped around so that the bow was over her ear, but Nonnie didn't even notice.

"Two," she said grandly, handing her money to the man by the side of the merry-go-round. When she got her ticket, she ran to find a giraffe. Then, at the last minute, she changed her mind and climbed onto a pink camel.

There were other pink camels, and Kate thought maybe it would be like living in Africa to ride a camel. But she chose the yellow elephant instead. That was like being in Africa, too.

Kate sat on her elephant and watched the other children buying their tickets and climbing up on the merry-go-round animals. When everybody was ready, the music began. Slowly, slowly, the yellow elephant began to move up and down on his shiny pole. Then faster and faster. Kate was so happy and excited she forgot all about her poor little 2$ Special, with the hands pointing to eight minutes past ten. She forgot that Mr. Not So Much was coming back in a week to check up on her, and she forgot that Elsie May was going to tell on her for going to the carnival without asking Miss Lavender and Miss Plum.

Kate forgot everything except the beautiful yellow elephant and the music and the thrill of seeing the carnival spread out all around as she came whizzing by. Game booths, food booths, balloons, colored flags

fluttering. Kate could see the whole carnival from the high back of the yellow elephant. Kate named him King, and she wished the music would never stop.

Round and round went the merry-go-round. Carousel music filled the summer morning. People waved to Kate on her yellow elephant named King. Round and round she went, and people waved to her. A new line was forming by the ticket-seller. Soon the yellow elephant began to move up and down more slowly. The music came to an end. The merry-go-round stopped, and it was time to get off.

"Good-bye, King," Kate whispered to the beautiful yellow elephant. She was the last one to leave the merry-go-round. Already, new children were crowding on, choosing the animals they would ride.

Finally Kate could linger no longer, and she went toward the man who was calling, "This way off, please. This way off."

Nonnie was waiting.

"What took you so long?"

She didn't really wait for Kate to answer. "Come on," she said eagerly, "I want to win a doll. Let's find that booth where you toss rings. Three for a quarter the man said. Here, you can play, too."

Nonnie unscrewed the lid of her money jar and put a quarter in Kate's hand. "Come on, let's find that booth."

Kate thought she would rather spend her quarter for another ride on the merry-go-round, and she stood for a moment watching the children who were riding now. A boy with a baseball cap was riding King.

When Kate turned around to follow Nonnie, Nonnie was nowhere in sight. People milled around, and the roly-poly man selling lemonade came by — but Nonnie was nowhere to be seen.

Kate turned this way and that.

"Nonnie!" she called. "Nonnie — Nonnie — where are you?"

What Time Is It?

✳ Kate began to feel panicky. How could she find Nonnie in the crowd of people at the carnival? She had no idea which way Nonnie had gone. And what time was it? Maybe it was time to get back to The Good Day for lunch. Kate wanted to be on time. *Now you have your watch,* Mr. Not So Much had said. *You need never be late again.*

Kate looked at the 2$ Special desperately. She shook her arm to see if she could get it started. But the hands still pointed to eight minutes past ten.

Kate wanted to run right back to Butterfield Square, whatever time it was, and hope that she was not late for lunch.

But it didn't seem right to go off without Nonnie. Kate stood on tiptoe and tried to see over the other people. But wherever she looked, she could not see Nonnie with her skinny knees and elbows, and her purple hair ribbon.

"Please — could you tell me what time it is?" Kate asked two girls who came hurrying by. But the girls didn't even hear Kate over all the noise and the music of the merry-go-round.

"Please — could you tell me what time it is?" Kate asked a woman who was carrying a bunch of balloons in one hand and a stuffed toy rabbit in the other.

"I'm sorry, I don't have my watch on," the woman said kindly. She hurried on before Kate could ask her if she knew where the ring-toss booth was.

Suddenly a voice quite near began to call, "Step right up, ladies and gentlemen. One quarter to see the marvelous powers of

Mr. Mysterious. He knows all, sees all, and — ha ha ha — sometimes tells all, but not always — ha ha ha."

A tall thin man in a red vest and a straw hat stood by the entrance to a purple tent with a gold fringe. He spotted Kate and bent down, peering into the dark eyes under the strands of brown hair that fell across Kate's forehead.

"How about you, girlie? Only a quarter to see the great Mr. Mysterious."

"What time is it?" Kate asked anxiously. She didn't care about anything else now, not even the great Mr. Mysterious.

"What was that, girlie?" The man in the straw hat bent down closer to Kate and cupped a hand around his ear. "Speak up."

"Do you know what time it is?" Kate spoke up. She practically shouted.

"Ha ha ha." The man straightened up and began to laugh. "Mr. Mysterious is the one who knows all. One quarter to see his amazing powers at work."

And he plucked up Kate's quarter in his freckled fingers.

"But I only want to know what time it is —"

"Exactly, exactly — right this way."

The man swept open the flap of the tent and motioned Kate to step inside.

"Can I have my quarter back?"

"Ha ha ha," said the man, as the tent flap fell closed again behind Kate.

Mr. Mysterious

✳ The inside of the purple tent was not very large and not very brightly lit.

At a small round table sat a man in a long purple robe. He wore a silver crown on his head, and he had a short, pointed black beard.

"Come in, little one," he said, although Kate was already in. "Learn the mysteries of the universe. See the future. Share my secrets."

Kate felt a little nervous to hear all this about the mysteries of the universe. In the dim light of the purple tent, the bright, merry carnival seemed far away. Kate could only faintly hear the merry-go-round music.

"I just want to know what time it is," she said as bravely as she could.

Mr. Mysterious looked at Kate with mild surprise. "The time? Surely you want to know something more special than that."

"I want to find Nonnie," Kate said timidly, "but maybe I don't have time. Maybe I should start back right now."

"Back where?" Mr. Mysterious narrowed his eyes and looked at Kate.

"Back for lunch," Kate said. She thought that explained everything very well.

"Ah." Mr. Mysterious nodded and rubbed his bearded chin. "Lunch. I'm feeling a bit hungry myself, now that you mention it."

Kate stared at Mr. Mysterious unhappily. If he felt hungry, it was probably lunch time, and she would be late. She would have to leave Nonnie and run home alone ... but she didn't want to leave Nonnie.

Mr. Mysterious began to smile. "I see you have a watch, my dear," he said. "Perhaps you should consult it if you wish to know the time."

"It doesn't work," Kate explained. She held out her arm for Mr. Mysterious to look at her watch.

"Eight past ten?" Mr. Mysterious shook his head. "No, that's not right at all. It's eleven-thirty." He pulled back the sleeve of his flowing robe, and there was a shiny wristwatch.

"Your watch is more than an hour off," he told Kate.

"And it doesn't tick anymore either," Kate added.

"Hmmm." Mr. Mysterious looked at the 2$ Special doubtfully. "Doesn't tick either. That's a pity, isn't it."

"Can you fix watches?" Kate asked.

Mr. Mysterious straightened his crown and stroked his beard again. His dark eyes rolled. He hated to admit that anything was beyond his powers, but he could not fix watches.

"I have a better idea," he said after a

moment. "I'll just make your watch into a magic watch. When you wear it, you will always know the correct time, no matter where the hands point. How's that? How does that sound to you?"

It sounded wonderful to Kate.

"Can you do that?"

Mr. Mysterious waved his hand to brush away such a foolish question.

"I can do anything, my dear. I am Mr. Mysterious."

"First," he continued, "you must give me the watch."

Kate unbuckled the 2$ Special and Mr. Mysterious took it in his hands. He had long, thin fingers, sparkling with rings. The watch disappeared as he closed his hands around it.

He mumbled some words that Kate did not understand. They sounded a little like "abbbjjjum - itjumm - fygyllllll," but not exactly.

Then Mr. Mysterious opened his long thin fingers, and there was Kate's watch. It

looked just the same as ever.

"Go ahead, put it on," Mr. Mysterious said.

Kate reached out slowly and picked up the 2$ Special. Was it really magic now? She buckled it on her wrist and stared at the face. The hands had not moved. But somehow Kate knew that the time was exactly twenty-five minutes to twelve. She had twenty-five minutes to find Nonnie, get back to Butterfield Square, wash her hands, comb her hair, and be in her chair at the dining room table.

"Oh, thank you!" Kate looked up at Mr. Mysterious happily. Just then the man in the straw hat opened the tent flap and peered in. Someone else had paid a quarter and was waiting outside to see Mr. Mysterious.

"This way out, girlie," the man in the straw hat said to Kate.

She had only time to say "Thank you," one more time. Mr. Mysterious smiled at her. He held up a thin finger and winked an eye. "This is our little secret," he said, and the man in the straw hat hustled Kate on her way.

On Time!

✳ Kate stood outside the tent, blinking in the sunlight. It was now twenty-three minutes to twelve, then twenty-two minutes to twelve, then twenty-one. She looked frantically in every direction for the sight of Nonnie and her money jar.

"Popcorn — fresh buttered popcorn here!" A man as big as a giant, Kate thought, lumbered by. From white straps over his shoulder hung a big box filled with bags of popcorn. "Popcorn — fresh buttered pop-corn here!"

Oh, where was Nonnie?

And then, when Kate had almost given up hope, she saw Nonnie. And at the same moment, Nonnie saw Kate.

"I won a china dog!" Nonnie came running up to Kate, bursting with her news. She didn't know all the worry Kate had been through, looking for her.

They hurried along Willow Street and across the park in the Square. Kate was glad to see that Tatty and some of the other girls were still playing in the front yard. That meant that it wasn't quite lunch time yet. She looked at her watch. She knew it was ten minutes to twelve. The magic still worked, and she had plenty of time to run upstairs and tidy up. Kate was beginning to feel better and better. What had started out so badly had really been a pretty good morning.

She had gone to a carnival, and she had ridden on a yellow elephant.

She had a magic watch so she would never be late again.

Nonnie had won a china dog as big as a cookie jar.

Really, it had been a very good morning.

Miss Plum and Miss Lavender were waiting in the front hall. They had their hands folded and their mouths set in straight lines. The minute she saw Miss Plum and Miss Lavender, Kate felt her heart sink. She thought of her treasure box. It seemed like a boat that was drifting out to sea, drifting far away where she would never see it again.

"I won a china dog," Nonnie announced as soon as she saw the ladies. She didn't notice their folded hands and set mouths. "I won a china dog at the carnival."

"At the carnival?" Miss Plum asked with pretend politeness. "The carnival you did not ask permission to go to?"

Nonnie stood silently with her china dog and her glass jelly jar. Kate stood beside her. They could hear Elsie May snickering by the parlor doorway.

But it was hard for Miss Plum and Miss Lavender to scold Kate and Nonnie.

"Nonnie *is* allowed to go as far as Willow Street," Miss Lavender reminded Miss Plum when they learned where the carnival was.

"And she shared her money," Miss Plum added.

Both ladies thought that was a fine thing for Nonnie to do.

"And Kate is here in time for lunch." When Miss Plum said that, the matter was not ever spoken of again.

"Mr. Not So Much bought me a watch so I'll always be on time," Kate said.

"Isn't that a good idea." Miss Lavender beamed.

"A very good idea," Miss Plum said.

They did not ask to take a close look at the 2$ Special, and Kate didn't tell that it was now a magic watch. Mr. Mysterious had said it would be their secret.

"Can I have my treasure box now?" Kate asked, but Miss Plum shook her head.

"I'm afraid it is a little too soon for that, Kate," she said. She looked into Kate's disappointed face. "I'm glad you were on time for breakfast this morning. I'm glad you are on time for lunch. But I think we will have to wait a bit on the treasure box."

Every morning Kate was on time for breakfast. Every noon she was on time for lunch. Every evening she was on time for supper.

No more did Miss Plum look around the

table at twenty-seven girls and an empty chair at Kate's place.

On Saturday afternoon at three o'clock, Kate was on time for her piano lesson. "Five to three," she would think, looking at her watch. "Time to go."

Soon school would open for the fall term, and Miss Plum hoped that Kate would be on time for school. Just think — no more calling upstairs, no more of Kate's mad rushes out of the door when the other girls were already a block away. No more notes from teachers: KATE WAS LATE. Time would tell of course, but Miss Plum was hopeful.

The days went by, and Kate was never late to a meal. She was never late for anything. She even reminded the other girls sometimes when it was time for them to do something. She always knew exactly what time it was. She had magic to help her now.

The carnival was gone from Willow Street. It left the very day after Kate and Nonnie rode the merry-go-round, after Nonnie won the china dog, and Kate got her magic watch. The carnival was gone. Mr. Mysterious was gone.

Kate thought about him sometimes, but she never told anyone her secret. Every day she buckled the 2$ Special on her wrist. Its small hands still pointed faithfully to eight minutes past ten.

The Missing Watch

※ It was fun to always know what time it was. Kate began to notice clocks. She had never thought much about clocks before, or about time, either.

The parlor clock was in a brown wooden case that gleamed in the sunlight. Around the rim of the clock face was a thin circle of gold. The hands were made of gold — a long hand for the minutes and a short hand for the hours. It should be the other way around, Kate thought. Hours were certainly longer than minutes. It was like a little joke the clock was playing.

The kitchen clock was shaped like a teapot. It was on the wall by the stove. Cook always knew just what time it was when she was fixing meals.

Kate was admiring the teapot clock one afternoon when she was in the kitchen with Tatty and Little Ann. They were helping Cook make lemonade.

"You stir," Cook said. She gave Kate a long-handled spoon to stir ice cubes in the lemonade pitcher. As Kate took the spoon, she saw that she didn't have her watch on her wrist. Her heart plunged. The magic watch was gone.

"What's the matter?" Tatty asked. "You look sort of funny."

"I've lost my watch!"

"Ohhh." Little Ann made a sad little sound and gazed at Kate.

"Where is it, where is it?" Kate looked around the kitchen, but there was no magic watch anywhere to be seen. "Oh, how can I ever find it!" she wailed.

"Now stop a minute and think where

you've been." Cook's round good face was full of sympathy. "Think what you've been doing this afternoon. Retrace your steps and you can find the watch."

Tatty and Little Ann stood by, ready to help, but Kate shook her head. "I've been everywhere! I played tag all over the yard — and I skated around the block and through the park — and I went to the post office with Elsie May to get stamps for Miss Plum — and I hunted all over the cellar to find an empty flower pot for Miss Lavender — "

Cook looked a little dazed at this list of activities. Maybe it was not going to be that easy for Kate to retrace her steps and find her watch.

"You've done all that just today?" Cook asked.

"Just this afternoon," Kate said. "This morning I helped Nonnie look for money and we went *everywhere*. And then we went next door to see the kittens and we played in their yard — and then we — "

Cook held up her hands. She had heard

enough. There must be a better way to find the watch than to look everywhere that Kate had been in just one day. The yard alone would be quite a search. The watch was small and the summer grass thick.

"There must be a better way," Cook said. But she could not think of one.

Everybody looked at Kate silently. Little Ann made her sad little sound again.

Then Tatty brushed back her hair and said, "Maybe it's not really lost. Maybe you forgot to put it on this morning."

Kate started to shake her head. She never forgot to put on her watch, her wonderful magic watch. But Cook thought this was just the answer. "Run upstairs, Kate. See if your watch isn't right where you put it last night. I'll bet it is."

So they all ran off, Kate and Tatty and Little Ann. Halfway down the hall, three other little girls began to run with them, just to see what all the excitement was about. All six burst into Kate's room. There on the table by her bed, by the lamp, and a coloring book, was Kate's magic watch. Nobody knew it was magic but Kate, of course. But there was the watch. Safe and sound.

"We found your watch! We found your watch!" Little Ann began to clap her hands.

Kate buckled on the watch and went right back to the kitchen to show Cook. Tatty and Little Ann went with Kate, but the other girls drifted away to do other things. They didn't think finding your watch right by your very own bed where you had left it was such a great thing to be making all this commotion over.

"There, I told you so!" Cook exclaimed when she saw the watch. (She forgot she had said *"Retrace your steps."*) "Look in your room, I said, that's the place."

Kate took up the long-handled spoon and began to stir the lemonade again. She watched ice cubes clinking against the sides of the pitcher, but she was thinking about her magic watch. All day she had not even had it on and yet she had been on time for breakfast and she had been on time for lunch. She had practiced the piano in the morning and when the parlor clock had chimed ten she knew her half hour was over. She was beginning to notice Time.

Maybe she didn't really need to wear the watch every day. It was sort of in the way when she was trying to walk on her hands and climb trees and important things like that. And she was sometimes afraid she might break the glass over the face of the watch when she did cartwheels or walked the fence rail.

But she didn't want to take any chances. She wanted her treasure box back, and she wanted to be sure nothing went wrong.

The Gold Watch

✳ While Kate was stirring the lemonade and thinking about her magic watch, Mr. Not So Much arrived in Butterfield Square. Miss Plum saw him coming, and she opened the door as he came up the front walk. It was a day earlier than Mr. Not So Much had said he would return. No one was expecting him.

"Why, Mr. Not So Much," Miss Plum said. "This is a surprise."

"I was in the neighborhood." Mr. Not So Much stalked past Miss Plum and made his way to the parlor.

Miss Lavender was in the parlor. "Why, Mr. Not So Much," she said, trying to look pleased. "This is a surprise."

"Not so much fuss, not so much fuss," Mr. Not So Much said crossly. He could see there were caramel candies in a dish on the table — such wastefulness! But he had not come to check on money matters today and he shut them from his mind, though it was not easy.

"I've only come to see Kate," he said to Miss Plum. "I've been wondering how she is doing, now that she has her watch."

"Kate is doing splendidly," Miss Lavender spoke up quickly. She patted her white curls and smoothed her skirt. She had not been expecting anyone and she always liked to look tidy. "She is always on time for meals, and sometimes she even reminds the other girls when it is time for them to do something and they've forgotten."

"I'm glad to hear it," Mr. Not So Much said. He settled himself in a chair by the sofa and stretched his long legs out across the carpet before him.

"Send for her," he directed Miss Plum.

"I think she is out in the kitchen helping

Cook make lemonade," Miss Lavender said. And then she was sorry she had spoken up so quickly. Mr. Not So Much did not like to be reminded about things like lemonade. His idea of a cooling treat was a glass of water. It was practically free.

"Yes, I believe she is in the kitchen," Miss Plum said. "I'll get her right away."

"Hmmm," Mr. Not So Much growled to himself and closed his eyes wearily. Just as Miss Lavender suspected, he was disturbed to think of the cost of lemonade for twenty-eight thirsty girls. He was almost sorry he had stopped in.

Very quickly Miss Plum returned from the kitchen with Kate. Miss Plum sat down beside Miss Lavender on the sofa, and Kate stood in front of Mr. Not So Much. She was thinking of her narrow escape. Only a few minutes ago her watch had been upstairs on her bedside table. What if Mr. Not So Much had come then and seen that she was not wearing it?

"I have only a few minutes," Mr. Not So

Much began. Everybody was relieved to hear that. "At three-thirty I must leave for a meeting at the bank. I am never late to meetings. Time is money."

Kate rubbed one shoe on top of the other and waited. It was almost three-thirty already. Mr. Not So Much would soon be gone.

"Now," Mr. Not So Much continued, "I understand that you have mended your ways."

Kate said nothing. She could not sew a stitch, and she had never mended anything in her life. But she didn't want to disappoint Mr. Not So Much, so she remained silent.

"Miss Lavender tells me you are now on time for meals," Mr. Not So Much continued.

"Yes, sir."

"And she tells me you sometimes remind the other girls when it is time for them to do something and they have forgotten."

Kate smiled modestly.

Mr. Not So Much leaned back against the chair. He crossed his legs and studied Kate approvingly. Then he drew out his magnificent gold watch and consulted the time.

He slipped the watch back into his pocket and settled himself more comfortably, as though he meant to stay a while longer.

Kate thought this was strange, for it was now exactly three-thirty. She thought he should be getting up and putting on his hat. He should be getting ready to be on his way to the meeting at the bank — for which he was never late.

Mr. Not So Much turned to Miss Lavender and Miss Plum. Miss Plum was sitting very straight, her hands folded in her lap. Miss Lavender was sitting straight, too, but she was so plump and ruffly she never looked quite the same as Miss Plum.

"You see," Mr. Not So Much explained with a grand gesture of his hand, "the young lady only needed a watch. It was a simple solution."

Miss Lavender and Miss Plum smiled.

"I am surprised neither of you thought of it yourselves," Mr. Not So Much added, a little less warmly.

Miss Lavender dropped her eyes and picked at the button on her dress. Miss Plum's smile became somewhat tight-lipped, but she managed to reply politely. "Of course, Mr. Not So Much. I don't know why we didn't think of it."

Mr. Not So Much tapped his forehead with a bony finger, as if to say here in this head, in *his* head, were many wonderful ideas that did not come to other, lesser persons.

Miss Lavender missed this, because she was still studying her button, but Miss Plum saw and nodded. She wished Mr. Not So Much would go to his meeting and bother the people there instead.

At last Kate could be quiet no longer —

"Excuse me, sir," she blurted out. "It's past three-thirty. It's nearly five minutes past. Won't you be late for your meeting?"

Miss Plum silently breathed a sigh of relief and started to get up to see Mr. Not So Much to the door.

But Mr. Not So Much did not seem concerned. He drew out his pocket watch again and waved a finger at Kate.

"I have five minutes yet until three-thirty," he announced.

His eyes narrowed and he glanced sharply at Kate. "Is that what your watch says? Five minutes past three-thirty? Is your watch out of order already?"

Kate looked down at the 2$ Special. The hands still pointed to eight minutes past ten. But before she could answer, Miss Lavender exclaimed, "It must be past three-thirty. There goes Mr. Watson on his way to work. He always goes by just a little past three-thirty. We can almost set our clocks by him."

Everyone turned to look out of the parlor window. There, sure enough, was Mr. Watson walking by on his way to work.

"I wouldn't set any clocks by him today," Mr. Not So Much said impatiently. Nevertheless, he held his watch to his ear and shook it. He listened to it and frowned to himself.

Miss Plum looked at the mantel clock, but someone had forgotten to wind it. It had stopped at two-ten. No help there.

"Kate," Miss Plum said, "run to the kitchen and see what Cook's clock says. She is usually right, because she sets her clock by the radio every morning."

Kate sped off — though she knew it was already eight minutes past three-thirty.

Mr. Not So Much could not hear his watch ticking. He shook it and rapped it with his finger. But it refused to tick. Something had happened to his beautiful gold watch.

But he did not want to admit this. Instead he stood up with dignity — as much dignity as he could have while trying to hurry — and he clapped on his hat and picked up his gloves.

"Three-thirty, I must be on my way," he muttered. Before Miss Plum or Miss Lavender could rise, he was striding through the parlor doorway. He collided with Kate, who was running breathlessly from the kitchen to say that *now* it was twenty minutes to four!

But Mr. Not So Much did not give Kate time to say anything. With a slam of the front door, he was gone. From the parlor window Miss Plum and Miss Lavender could see him racing away at double speed.

"Why, I do believe Mr. Not So Much was having some trouble with his watch," Miss Lavender said. She began to giggle softly.

"I imagine he will be late to his meeting," Miss Plum said.

"And now Kate certainly has earned back

her treasure box," Miss Lavender said. She put her arm around Kate's shoulder and kissed her on the forehead.

"Yes, I think you are right, Miss Lavender," Miss Plum agreed. She opened her desk drawer and took out the shoe box with Kate's careful printing on the lid: MY TREASURE BOX.

Inside, the wooden top bumped against the brass doorknob, the one that Phoebe had never seen. The blue marbles clinked together. Kate took the box carefully and opened the cover. Yes, everything was safe and sound, just as it had been.

"I am very pleased, Kate," Miss Plum said. "You have shown great improvement this last week."

"You see, it's really very easy when you get into the habit. Isn't it, dear?" Miss Lavender said.

Kate was hardly listening. She was stroking her pink ribbon again ... for a whole week she had not felt its soft silky feeling in her fingers. She was looking at her marbles and her key ... and the beautiful brass doorknob.

MY
TREASURE
BOX

Miss Lavender's Poem

※ The following day Miss Lavender and Miss Plum were in the parlor. The mantel clock, which Miss Plum had remembered to wind, ticked toward lunchtime, and Miss Lavender said, "I've written a new verse about Kate. Mary isn't the only one who can write poems, you know." She looked very pleased with herself.

"Let me hear it," Miss Plum urged.

Miss Lavender rummaged around the table beside the sofa. At first she could find only scraps of mending thread and her tiny silver thimble.

"Ah, yes, here it is." She held up a slip of paper and began to read:

> *"Kate be early,*
> *Kate be late.*
> *Kate's on time*
> *And never makes you wait."*

"Very nice," Miss Plum said thoughtfully. "It doesn't have quite the lilt of Mary's poem, but it's well put, Miss Lavender. And what's more important, it's true."

Upstairs, Kate was washing her hands for lunch. It was almost twelve. Phoebe and Mary were having a tug-of-war with a big towel, and Tatty was trying to get her hair to stay back by rubbing it with a wet wash cloth. Everybody was hungry!

But before she went downstairs, Kate slipped back to her room and unbuckled the 2$ Special. She opened her treasure box and gently laid the magic watch inside. It would be there in case she ever needed it again, but it would be safer. Now she could have roller skate races, and climb over the fence, and do all the things she liked to do, without having to be careful of the watch.

The watch was a wonderful addition to her collection. Kate thought she must have the most marvelous treasure box anyone could have. A brass doorknob and a little china cat ... marbles and a magic watch....

Kate closed the box. She could hear Little Ann laughing on the stairs and voices in the hallway below. She could hear Elsie May clumping down to lunch demanding, "Who took my blue hairbow?" and Nonnie saying, "I just borrowed it for a little while."

The parlor clock was striking twelve.

Kate hurried downstairs after the other girls. She was in her place at the table just as Cook was coming through the kitchen door, carrying a tray of sandwiches and the first pitcher of milk.